AuthorHouse™ LLC
1663 Liberty Drive
Bloomington, IN 47403
www.authorhouse.com
Phone: 1-800-839-8640

Published by AuthorHouse 02/28/2014

ISBN: 978-1-4918-4585-1 (sc)
*   978-1-4918-4586-8 (e)*

Library of Congress Control Number: 2013923467

Any people depicted in stock imagery provided by Thinkstock are models,
and such images are being used for illustrative purposes only.
Certain stock imagery © Thinkstock.

For Jarod
a boy who loves dinosaurs

When you ask animals to eat
Strange problems can arise.
The elephants can't find a seat
Of elephantine size.

Giraffes have need of low, low chairs,
While field mice need real high ones.
The eels have trouble with the stairs;
Chimps always tease the lions.

The octopi won't say, "Please pass";
They're always rather grabby.
The fish can't even hold a glass;
The crabs are often crabby.

These little social oddities
(I'm sure you've seen your share)
Can bring a host right to his knees
And make him tear his hair.

The funniest I'll ever see
Of parties of this kind
Occurred when Jarod graciously
Asked dinosaurs to dine.

6

Now, Jarod liked a lot of beasts,
Large dinosaurs the most.
He'd often shared their Friday feasts
But had never been their host.

Deciding this was impolite,
He asked his Mum if he
Could have some friends come for the night
For dinner and TV.

"Of course, dear, they can come," said she;
"What would they like to eat?"
And Jarod, absentmindedly,
Said "Ferns and grass and meat."

She stared; she shrugged; she went and shopped,
Then dinner-time came round.
The doorbell rang, and something hopped
Through the door in one great bound.

When I say through the door, I mean
The door and not the doorway.
Though Jarod thought the entrance keen;
His Mum thought it a poor way.

10

The Stegosaurus said hello;
He swung his mighty tail.
Unhappily the piano
Was what his tail-spikes nailed.

The instrument gave out a sound,
An untuned symphony.
The Stegosaurus looked around
And said, "Oh pardon me."

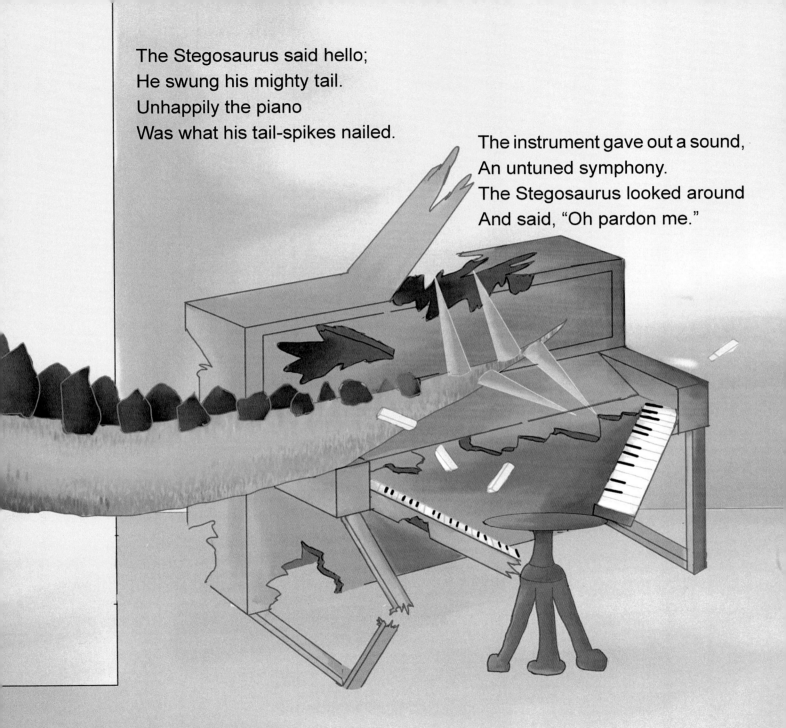

11

Politely, Jarod said, "No harm";
He smiled at him gaily.
But Mum took Jarod by the arm
And said, "Your friend looks. . . scaly."

"Of course!" cried Jarod, unabashed.
"He is a dinosaur!"
She looked at him, and then she crashed
Upon the kitchen floor.

She fainted dead away, you see.
(I'm not shocked in the least.)
She didn't think Jarod's friend would be
A prehistoric beast.

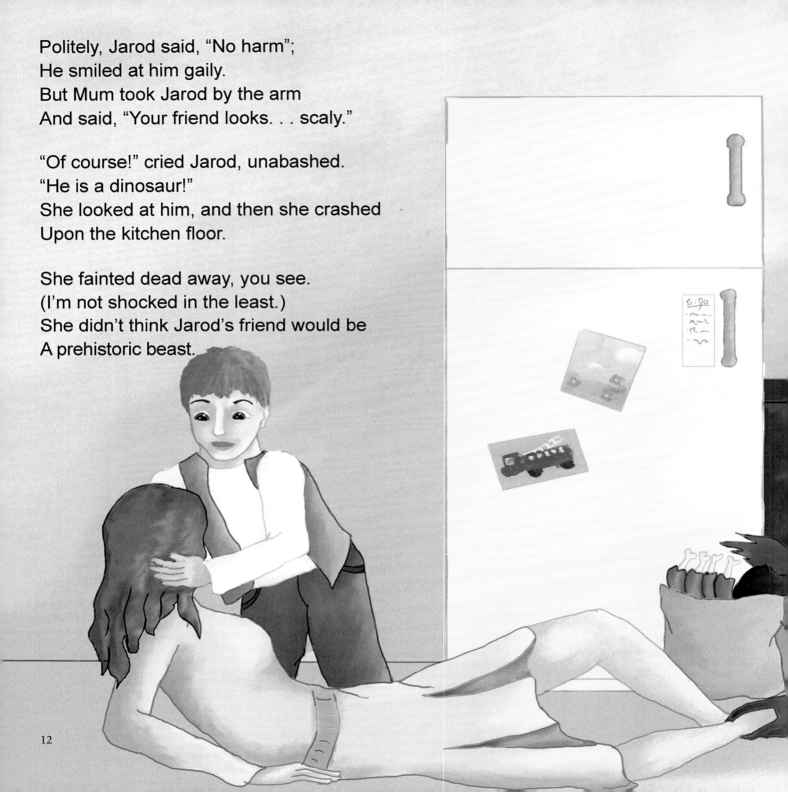

But Jarod raised his Mum right up
And smiled at his guest.
"Well, come right in," he said, "and sup;
Are ferns what you like best?"

The beast began to answer as
A foot came through the roof.
Tyrannosaurus entered thus;
It was his usual goof.

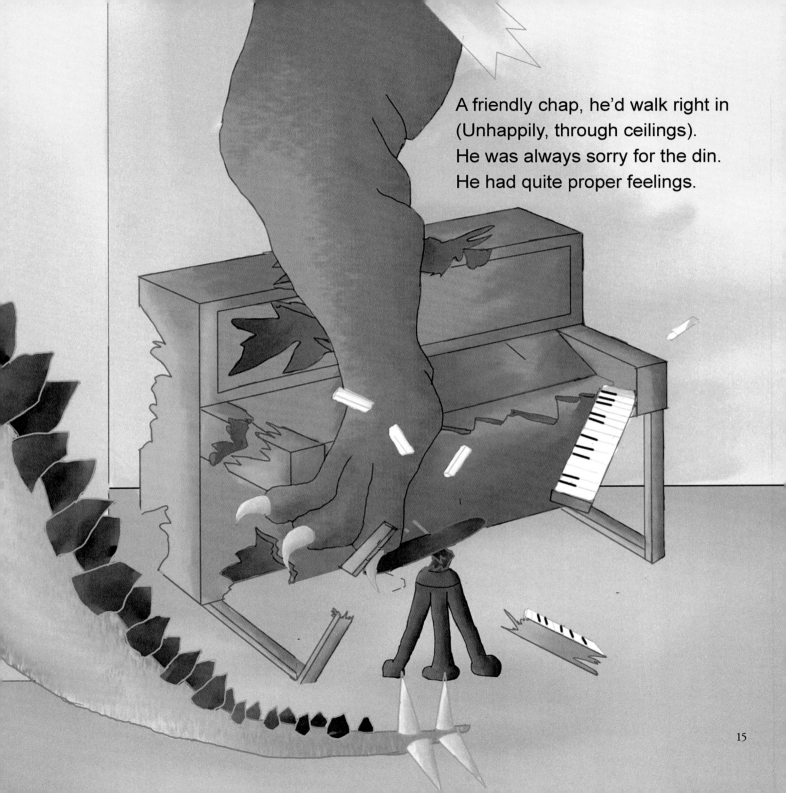

A friendly chap, he'd walk right in
(Unhappily, through ceilings).
He was always sorry for the din.
He had quite proper feelings.

15

Well, Jarod really understood.
The door was just too small.
So Jarod called, "Come in! Don't brood!
Just sit . . . upon that wall."

He passed the steaks; he passed the cakes;
Rex ate them in a bite.
Said Jarod, "He eats all he takes,
How wonderfully polite!"

Triceratops arrived in force;
He walked right through the casement.
His weight was too much for the floors;
He ended in the basement.

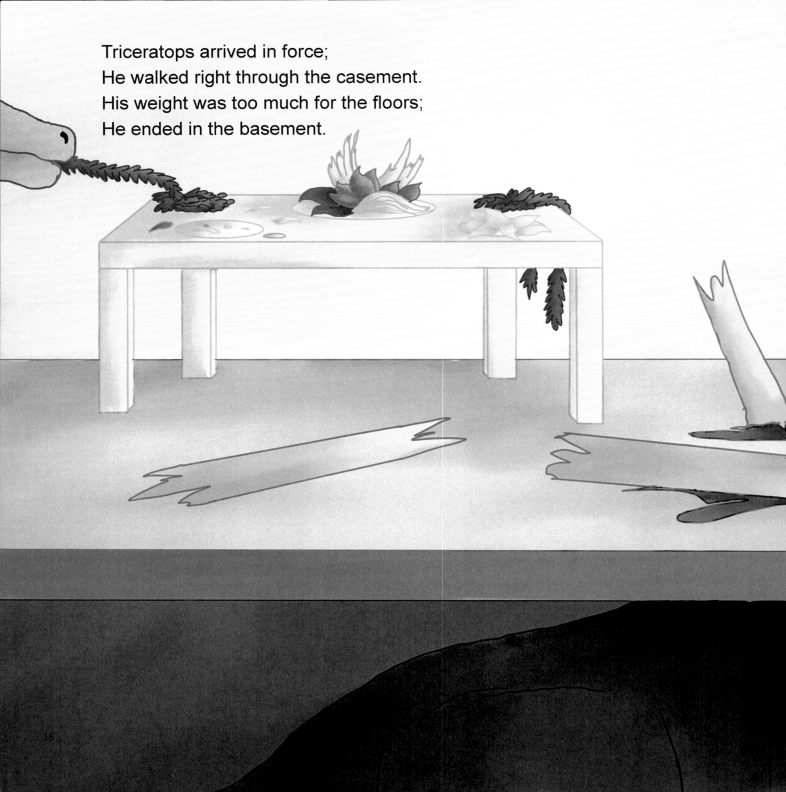

But he had manners, too, and said,
"I'm sorry for the mess!"
So Jarod patted his horned head
(Quite carefully, I guess).

Apatosaurus came, and he,
Though dainty as a mouse,
Made problems for the family:
He was bigger than the house.

Eventually he settled (BOOM!)
And asked for a cold soda.
His head stuck out through Jarod's room;
His tail pierced the Toyota.

He apologized (he was well bred):
"I'm sorry! Oh, poor car!"
Kind Jarod tried to pat his head
But couldn't reach that far.

They talked and ate till time for bed.
They had a lovely night.
"Oh, thank you so much!" each one said,
Then waddled out of sight.

Then Jarod cried, "I like them so!
I know they really tried!
They do make problems, though, I know.
Next time we'll eat outside."

Made in the USA
Middletown, DE
21 May 2015